FIRST FAIRY TALES

Puss in Boots

For Natalie – *MM*

For Big Oliver – *PN*

Series reading consultant: Prue Goodwin,
Reading and Language Information Centre,
University of Reading

Orchard Books
96 Leonard Street, London EC2A 4XD
Orchard Books Australia
Unit 32/45-51 Huntley Street, Alexandria, NSW 2015
This text was first published in Great Britain in the form
of a gift collection called *First Fairy Tales*,
illustrated by Selina Young, in 1994
This edition first published in Great Britain in hardback in 2005
First paperback publication 2006
Text © Margaret Mayo 1994
Illustrations © Philip Norman 2005
The rights of Margaret Mayo to be identified as the author and
Philip Norman to be identified as the illustrator have been
asserted by them in accordance with the
Copyright, Designs and Patents Act, 1988.
A CIP catalogue record for this book is available from the British Library
ISBN 1 84362 452 4 (hardback)
ISBN 1 84362 454 0 (paperback)
1 3 5 7 9 10 8 6 4 2 (hardback)
1 3 5 7 9 10 8 6 4 2 (paperback)
Printed in Hong Kong, China

FIRST FAIRY TALES
Puss in Boots

Margaret Mayo ⭐ Philip Norman

ORCHARD BOOKS

In an old windmill on top of a hill, there once lived a poor man and his three sons.

When the poor man died, he left the windmill to the eldest son,

the donkey to the second,

and the third got Puss – the family cat.

The youngest son was disappointed. "I am fond of you, Puss," he said, "but you're not very useful. Except for catching mice!"

Puss looked up, and he said, "Get me a bag and a pair of boots, and I'll show you what I can do!"

So, the lad quickly found a bag, and his own best, soft leather boots.

Puss pulled on the boots, and they *s-h-r-a-n-k* until they fitted perfectly.

Then, he rose up on his hind legs, slung the bag over his shoulder and marched off.

When he came to a field where there were rabbit holes, he picked dandelion leaves, stuffed them in the bag and made a rabbit trap. Before long, a plump rabbit hopped into the bag and began to eat the leaves.

Clever Puss quickly closed the bag and slung it over his shoulder. Then, off he marched to the royal palace and gave the rabbit to the king.

"Your Majesty," said Puss, bowing low, "here is a present from my master, the Duke of Carabas."

And the king said, "I thank your master, the Duke of Carabas."

Then, off went Puss with the empty bag.

Next morning, Puss marched off again. When he came to a cornfield, he picked corn, dropped it in the bag and made a partridge trap.

And clever Puss caught two plump partridges...and took them to the king.

The next morning, Puss said to the youngest son, "Come with me. Do exactly what I tell you and I'll make your fortune!"

So they marched off, until they came to a river that flowed past the royal palace.

"This afternoon," said Puss, "the king is going for a drive with his beautiful daughter. You shall meet her – then marry her. Now, take off those old clothes and go for a swim!"

"All right, Puss!" said the lad.
And he took off his clothes and
jumped in the river. Then, Puss
stuffed everything into his bag and
hid it under a large stone.

As soon as the royal carriage appeared, Puss waved and shouted, "Help! Help!"

When the king saw the strange cat who had brought him presents, he stopped the carriage.

"Your Majesty," said Puss, "while my master, the Duke of Carabas, was swimming, thieves stole ALL his clothes."

"He has no clothes!" exclaimed the king. "That won't do." And he ordered a servant to fetch some new clothes from the palace.

When the servant returned with the clothes, the lad climbed out of the river and put them on. Then, he looked so handsome and grand, just like a real duke!

He bowed to the king and the beautiful princess and said, "Your Majesty, thank you for your kindness."

"And I thank you, Duke of Carabas, for your presents," said the king. "Now, will you join us for a ride in the country?"

So the lad climbed into the carriage, and they were off.

And Puss – what about him?
He ran ahead until he came to
a huge cornfield where men were
busy cutting the corn.

Puss knew that the field
belonged to a fierce ogre.

But he shouted, "Listen! When the king comes by, tell him that the field and land round about belong to the Duke of Carabas. If you don't, I SHALL CHOP YOU INTO MINCE MEAT!"

When the royal carriage came
bowling along and the king saw
the huge cornfield, he called out,
"Who owns this field?"

And the men sang out, "The field and land round about belong to the Duke of Carabas!"

The king thought, "*Hmmm...* this duke must be rich!"

And Puss – what about him?
He ran ahead until he came to the
ogre's castle. He knocked at the
door. *Bam! Bam! Bam!*

The door swung open, and
there stood the ogre. He was
ENORMOUS!

"Mighty Ogre," said Puss, "I have heard that you are a great magician and can change into an elephant...a lion...anything!"

"True!" said the ogre.

And...*vroom!* he was a lion.

Puss was so scared that he raced
inside and jumped on to a table.

Then...*vroom!* the lion was an
ogre again.

"Amazing!" said Puss. "But can
you change into a tiny animal, like
a mouse? That must be impossible
for an enormous ogre!"

"IMPOSSIBLE?" bellowed the ogre. He was angry.

And...*vroom!* he was a mouse running across the floor.

Puss was quick. One big leap and he caught the mouse...and gobbled him up!

A few moments later, Puss heard
the sound of carriage wheels, so he
hurried outside. He bowed and
said, "Welcome to the castle
of my master, the Duke
of Carabas!"

The king looked up at the huge castle and he thought, "*Hmmm…* this duke must be *very* rich!"

Then Puss led everyone into the castle. It was full of treasures and the king thought, "*Hmmm…*this duke must be *very, very* rich!"

He said, "Duke of Carabas, would you like to marry my daughter?"

The lad looked at the beautiful princess, and she smiled. So he asked her to marry him. And after that, there was a wedding!

And clever Puss in Boots – what about him? He lived for many happy years in the ogre's castle with his master and the beautiful princess. He had his own velvet cushion by the fire, plenty of saucers full of cream and lots of other tasty treats!

FIRST FAIRY TALES
by Margaret Mayo
Illustrated by Philip Norman

Enjoy a little more magic with these other First Fairy Tales:

❏ Cinderella	1 84121 150 8	£3.99
❏ Hansel and Gretel	1 84121 148 6	£3.99
❏ Jack and the Beanstalk	1 84121 146 X	£3.99
❏ Sleeping Beauty	1 84121 144 3	£3.99
❏ Rumpelstiltskin	1 84121 152 4	£3.99
❏ Snow White	1 84121 154 0	£3.99
❏ The Frog Prince	1 84362 457 5	£3.99
❏ Puss in Boots	1 84362 454 0	£3.99

Animal Crackers
by Rose Impey
Illustrated by Shoo Rayner

Have you read any Animal Crackers?

❏ A Birthday for Bluebell	1 84121 228 8	£3.99
❏ Hot Dog Harris	1 84121 232 6	£3.99
❏ Tiny Tim	1 84121 240 7	£3.99

and many other titles.

First Fairy Tales and Colour Crackers are available from all good bookshops,
or can be ordered direct from the publisher:
Orchard Books, PO BOX 29, Douglas IM99 1BQ
Credit card orders please telephone 01624 836000
or fax 01624 837033
or e-mail: bookshop@enterprise.net for details.

To order please quote title, author and ISBN
and your full name and address.
Cheques and postal orders should be
made payable to 'Bookpost plc'.
Postage and packing is FREE within the UK
(overseas customers should add £1.00 per book).

Prices and availability are subject to change.